The ghost says
this book belongs to

_____

_____

Published by:
Timothy Falcon Crack, P.O. Box 6385,
Dunedin North, Dunedin 9059, New Zealand

First published January 2016
Revised March 2016

ISBN: 978-0-9941182-6-4

The authors thank
John G. Keller for his generous advice
and Marianne Lown for careful editing.

Typeset by the publisher.
Printed in the U.S.A., U.K., and Australia
www.MeteorMalcolm.com

GHOSTS

Malcolm Crack
Timothy Crack

This is a ghost.

There are many
different kinds
of ghosts.

Some
ghosts
are
tall.

Some ghosts
are short.

Some ghosts are plump.

Some ghosts are skinny.

These are
the lungs
of a ghost.

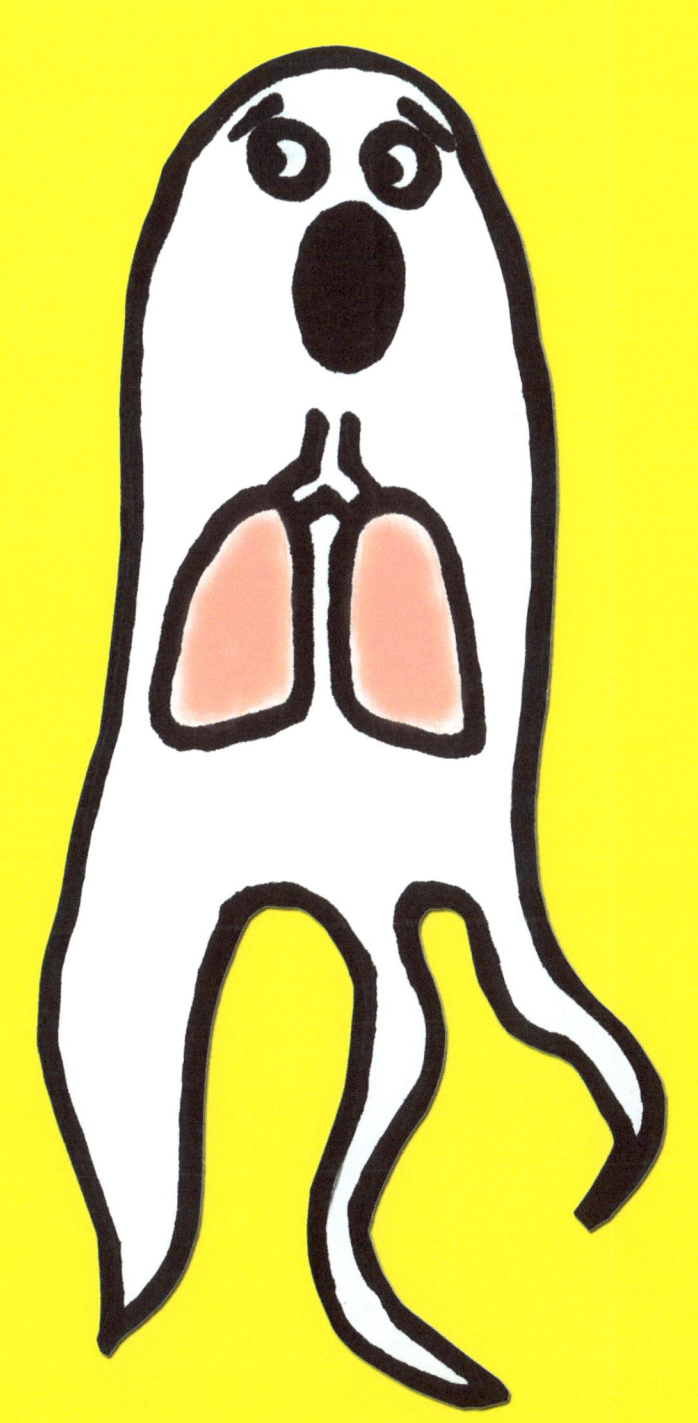

Some ghosts are funky.

Some ghosts
are scary...

...even to
other ghosts.

Some ghosts are
scared of you!

Ghosts can fly!

Some ghosts
are crazy.

Some ghosts
are friendly.

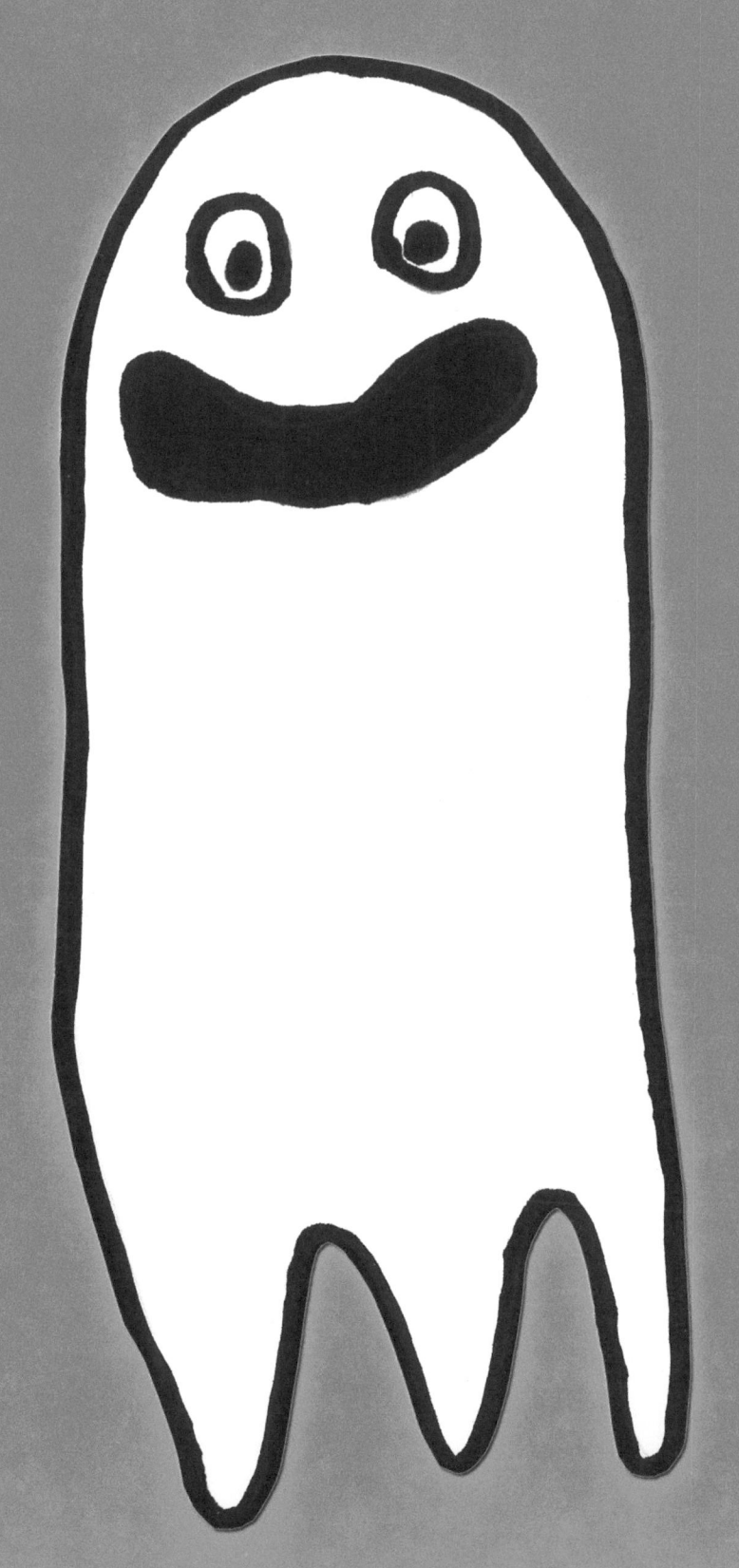

Ghosts can be colorful.

This ghost is
almost invisible.

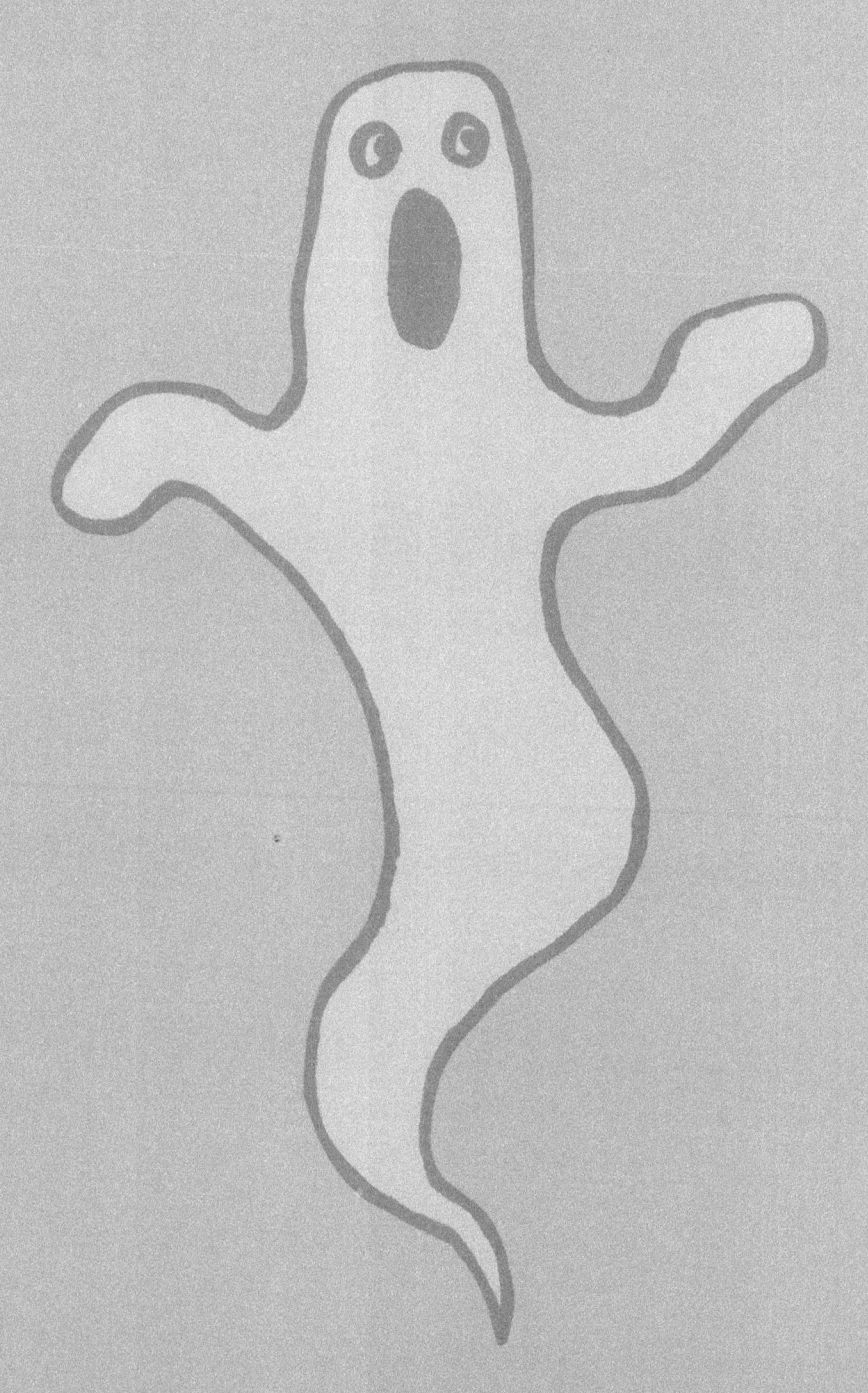

There can be
ghosts of animals.

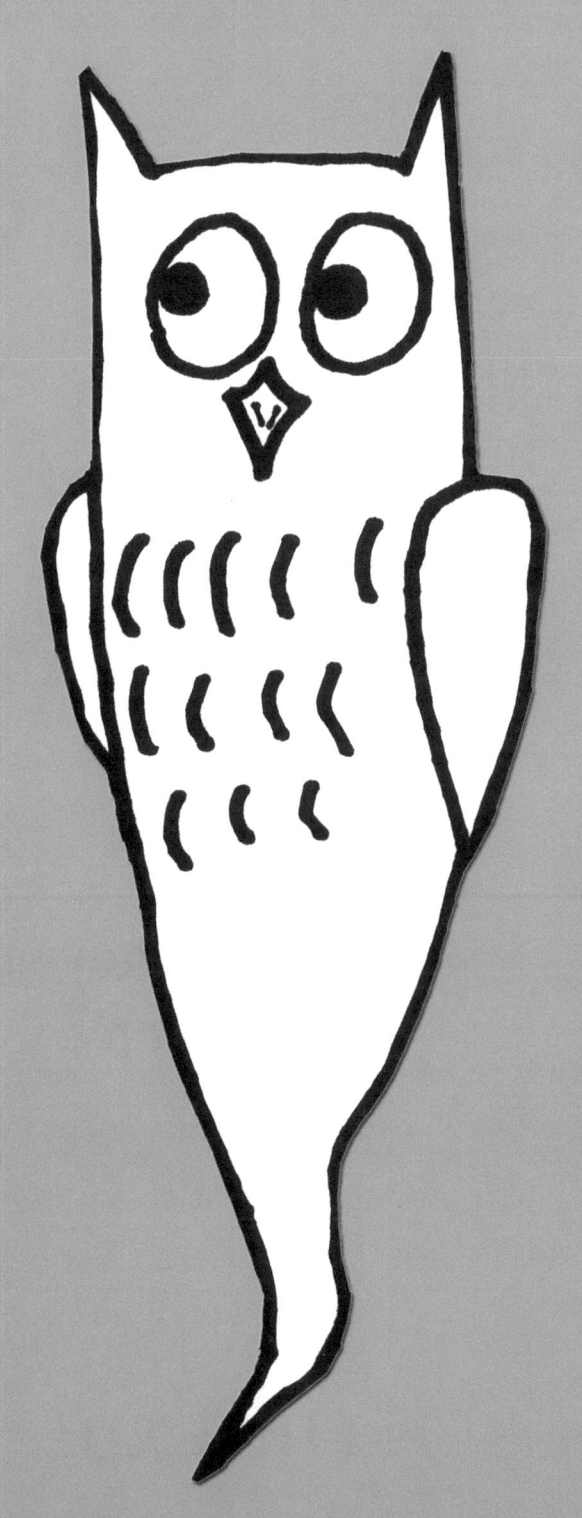

Some ghosts
like to stay
up late and
look at the stars...

...but they get
sleepy.

THE END

QUESTIONS:

Can you find
FIVE friendly ghosts?

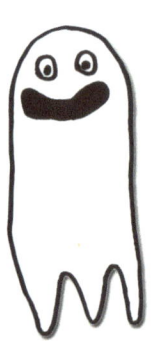

Can you find
THREE blue ghosts?

Can you find
ONE ghost who is
scared of YOU?

Which were your
FAVORITE ghosts
in the book?

HOW TO DRAW A GHOST

Step 1: Face

Step 2: Top

Step 3: Bottom...

...or a different bottom

Step 4: Eyebrows, Hair, Color, or add whatever you want!